COLD CUT MURDER

THE DARLING DELI SERIES, BOOK 3

PATTI BENNING

SUMMER PRESCOTT BOOKS PUBLISHING

ONE

Moira Darling stood outside with her hands on her hips, assessing the huge banner that read *Welcome to the Annual Maple Creek Winter Festival.* Candice and Darrin were hanging it in the window of her deli, Darling's DELIcious Delights, and depending on her to tell them when it was evenly centered in the front of the store. After a moment, she gave them a thumbs up and headed back inside to congratulate them. The banner had taken them the better part of the morning to create, and it had been a pain to get it hung straight across the front window. But now, thanks to the hard work of her employees, the deli was beginning to look ready for the biggest tourist event of the season.

"What else do we have left to do, Mom?" Candice asked once Moira had gotten inside and stomped the snow off her boots.

"I was thinking we could hang some paper snowflakes like we did last year, and we can put some red and pink lights out for Valentine's Day. Plus, of course, all the extra cooking. Are you sure you still want to be in charge of the cookies?" She didn't doubt that her daughter could handle it, but she knew from experience that making enough cookies would be hard work. The deli didn't usually serve any freshly made foods other than soups, salads, and sandwiches, but one of the local churches did a charity drive every year during the Winter Festival, and all of the small businesses joined in. Most of the proceeds from the cookies would be donated, and last year alone the deli had sold a few hundred of them on the busiest day.

"Definitely," her daughter replied. "You'll have enough on your plate without having to worry about that, too."

"Just make sure you leave yourself enough time to do something fun. I heard that they're actually hiring a live band for the Valentine's dance this year," she said. She herself hadn't gone to the dance for a few years, but she knew her daughter loved that sort of thing.

"Don't worry, I wouldn't miss the dance for anything," Candice said with a grin. She looked like she was about to say something else, but whipped her head around and gasped when something in the deli's kitchen began a high-pitched beeping.

"Oh, the fudge is ready," she exclaimed. "You two wait here—you've got to try it!"

Moira and Darrin both tried not to laugh as the young woman ran into the kitchen to check on the state of her fudge. Her daughter had recently declared that her dream was to open a candy shop, and she had been experimenting with recipes for the last few weeks. Most of what she made was quite good, but there had been a few questionable results. Luckily, everyone who worked at the deli was more than happy to taste test Candice's experiments— after all, they were used to Moira using them as guinea pigs for new soup recipes.

While her daughter cut the fudge into manageable pieces in the back, the deli owner began straightening the food on the refrigerated shelves, and

Darrin rang up a customer at the register. Besides the daily special, which in the winter was usually soup and a sandwich, the deli also sold a variety of fresh cheeses, meats, sauces, and even fruit and vegetable drinks. Moira was proud of the fact that everything she sold was from local farmers and small businesses. Her store was the only one like it in town, and she usually kept up a pretty good stream of business even in the off season. When the weather warmed up and tourists began visiting the small town, she knew that she and her employees would be busier than ever.

"Moira, I'm glad I caught you before you closed for the day," a familiar voice rang out. She straightened and looked around to see Martha, a woman her own age who was quickly becoming a close friend.

"It's nice to see you," she replied with a smile. "Are you stopping by for something in particular, or just to say hi?"

"Oh, a bit of both," her friend said. "I've got some news you might want to hear, plus I couldn't resist seeing what your special is today. You always have the best food."

"Well, today we've got split pea and ham soup, and toasted Italian bread sandwiches with cold cuts, ham, bacon, onion, and lettuce," she said, gesturing to the small blackboard next to the register.

"Isn't that the soup that the food critic refused to finish?" Martha asked, raising her eyebrows.

"You remember that, do you?" Moira shook her head. "That man was a joke. He said that the soup was too chunky, and he hated the pieces of ham in it. Enough other people told me that they loved it that I decided not to change the recipe, but I'll definitely be serving him something else if he comes back this year." During the Winter Festival, the year before, a food critic had come to town to try out the food at each local business. She didn't think that he had given any place in town more than three stars.

"I'll take a bowl of it; I don't need some strange man to tell me what's good food and what isn't."

She followed the deli owner to the register, where another customer was just finishing up an order. He gave Moira a nervous smile when she saw him. *He looks familiar*, she thought. She realized that she'd seen the same guy each day this week. She returned his smile; it looked like she had a new regular.

"You shouldn't even let him in if he comes back this year," Martha continued as she waited in line. "Bad reviews from a food critic might not mean much to the locals, but it could make an impact on the tourists."

"I don't think I can just deny him service," she pointed out. "Besides, I don't think the opinions of one unfair critic will be too bad for business."

"I hope not," her friend said. She paused while the man in front of her gathered up his food and moved out of the way before continuing, "Oh, that actually brings me to my other news. I'm sure you heard that the guy who bought the Soup Shoppe shut down the one in town?"

"I sure did," Moira said as she keyed in the other woman's order and rang her up. "It was in the paper a few weeks ago. I've gotten a few of my customers back, which is nice."

"Well, someone is opening *another* restaurant there," Martha told her. "I think it's some sort of steakhouse."

"That'll be great; I won't have to drive to Lake Marion if I want a nice dinner."

"But... aren't you worried about the competition?" her friend asked, surprised by Moira's calm attitude.

"Not really," she said. "A steakhouse will actually be less competition than the Soup Shoppe was; I don't serve steaks, after all."

"I suppose," her friend said with a shrug. "One more thing. Are you going to that dance they have in City Hall every year?"

"I wasn't planning on it," Moira said.

"Well, I know a guy who might like to take you. His name is Marcus, and he's from Lake Marion. I went on a few dates with his cousin. He seems nice, if you're interested." Martha smiled and raised an eyebrow. "Unless you've got someone else in mind to go with?"

Moira immediately thought of David Morris, the good-looking private investigator she had met a few months before and blushed. "I really wasn't planning on going at all. I'm too old for that sort of thing."

"Nonsense." Her friend patted her hand reassuringly. "Just think about it, all right?"

After promising that she would indeed think about it, Moira excused herself for a moment to duck into the kitchen and serve up a to-go bowl of the split pea soup. Candice was just finishing up with the fudge, and she handed her mother a piece. Moira was happy when the creamy chocolate fudge melted in her mouth; it was delicious.

"Do you mind if I give Martha a piece of this?" she asked her daughter. "It's amazing. Some of the best fudge I've ever had, in fact."

"Thanks, Mom." Her daughter grinned at her. "Sure, I'll wrap some up for her. Tell her I'll be right out."

After Martha left, the three of them began the familiar routine of closing up the deli. The extra soup was poured into to-go containers; she gave Darrin half and took the rest for herself. Most nights, she and Candice ate leftovers from the deli for dinner, but she made a point of cooking something new or going out to eat at least once a week. Tonight, looked like it would be a soup night though; the pea soup hadn't sold as well as she had expected. Maybe Martha was right; maybe the food critic was worse for business than she had thought.

TWO

The next day, she and Dante were the only ones scheduled to work, although Candice would be stopping in later with the first batch of cookies. Moira was at the deli at least six days a week, and sometimes worked whole months without a single day off. She was devoted to the store, and her hard work had paid off; she was making a good living for herself and could even help support her daughter in chasing her dreams.

She usually got to the deli an hour or so before it was supposed to open so that she could get the soup of the day simmering away and ready to be served to hungry customers, but since today was Sunday—the first day of the week-long Winter Festival—she knew that she would have even more work than usual to do. Normally in the off-season she only offered one soup each day and suggested a sandwich to go with it, but this week, to cater to the differing tastes of the visitors, she would be making multiple soups each day in addition to offering hot apple cider and cookies. The Winter Festival was important to the whole town, both because of its long tradition and the financial boost it gave the tourist town during the slow days of winter.

She got started on the first soup, a simple beef and veggie soup. Once the beef broth was simmering away, she dumped in sliced carrots, pearl onions, freshly snapped green beans, and cubed golden potatoes. She was in the middle of slicing the thick chunk of beef when she heard a knock at the deli's front door. *That's odd*, she thought, freezing mid-slice with the knife gripped tightly in her hand. She had learned caution over the last few months after two people she knew had been murdered. She used to think that Maple Creek was a safe town where nothing bad ever happened. Now she knew otherwise; bad things could happen no matter where you were.

The person knocked again, so she set down the knife and quickly washed her hands in the kitchen sink. She wasn't expecting any deliveries today, and her daughter and employees all had keys to let themselves in. Anyone else that she knew would either call her, or just wait until the deli was open to visit.

She was surprised to see the man from yesterday at the front door—the one that had been there while she and Martha had been talking. He was tall, with sandy blond hair and glasses, and seemed almost constantly nervous. She didn't know his name, but he seemed to be her newest regular.

"I'm sorry," she said when she unlocked and opened the front door. "We aren't open yet, but please come back in a few hours."

"Oh, I was actually hoping to talk to you," he said, looking down at the snow covered sidewalk. "I saw your car in the parking lot, and thought you might be less busy if I talked to you now, before the deli is open."

"Well, I've got soup on the stove, so I don't have long." She hesitated, then decided to let the man in. "What's your name?" she asked as she stepped aside so he could pass her. "I know I've seen you a few times, but I don't think I've managed to catch it."

"Steven," he told her. "And I know yours already. Thanks for letting me come in, Moira."

"It's nice to meet you," she said. "What did you want to talk to me about?" *Maybe they sent a different food critic this year,* she thought. But no, it wouldn't make sense for him to eat at her restaurant so often without telling her, and besides, the food critic didn't usually come until the Winter Festival had started— this man had been coming in all week.

"I... I wanted to know if you would like to go to the dance with me," he said, mumbling the first part of the sentence, then saying the last part so quickly that she almost didn't catch it. It took Moira a moment to realize that he meant the Valentine's dance. She blinked, not sure what to say.

"I'm sorry," she told him. "I don't think I'm going to go this year, plus I don't know you well enough to accept an invitation like that." She gave him a gentle smile, hoping that he couldn't see how uncomfortable she was.

"The dance isn't until next Sunday," he told her. "You have a whole week to get to know me. Don't you think you might change your mind?" *Is he really arguing with me to try to get me to go on a date with him?* she wondered.

"I'm just not interested. Sorry," she said. She pulled the deli's front door open again, letting a blast of icy air in. "Thanks for asking me though, and I do really appreciate your business. I hope to see you again while we're open." When he didn't move right away, she began to be worried that he was going to try to argue with her more, but after a second or two he huffed and walked through the open door, leaving without saying a word or looking back.

Moira was shaken by the incident, and decided to call her friend. As soon as she finished preparing the beef soup, she pulled out her phone and dialed Martha. It only took her a few minutes to relate the story, and she found that just telling someone else about it made her feel better.

"He just seemed sort of strange," she told her friend. "And he was pretty upset that I said no."

"I think it's sweet," Martha said. "He has obviously liked you for a while, if he's been coming to the deli and buying stuff just for a chance to see you."

"Do you think I should have agreed to go with him?" she asked.

"I mean, not necessarily with him, but I think you might have fun if you go to the dance. You haven't dated for a while, have you?"

"No," Moira admitted. "I just don't have the time."

"You should make time," her friend told her. "I'm sure there are plenty of guys that would be happy to go to the dance with you."

"Oh, I don't know about that," Moira said with a laugh. "Thanks for the vote of confidence, though."

"Any time," Martha said. "That's what friends are for, isn't it?"

THREE

The first day of the Winter Festival turned out to be a busy one at the deli. Moira was beginning to wish that she had scheduled more workers than just Dante and herself, but Darrin and Candice had come in early the day before to help her decorate; besides, her daughter was busy making cookies. It was nice to see a long line of customers at her register, and as long as Dante was willing to switch places with her every now and then, she was happy to work through the day without a break.

Candice stopped by shortly after the lunch rush with two platters full of sugar cookies, some decorated like snowflakes, others with a Valentine's Day theme. Moira was impressed with what her daughter had managed to bake in such a short time; she herself had never been one for baking cookies—desserts weren't her forte.

"Do you need me to stay, Mom, or do you want me to get started on tomorrow's cookies?" her daughter asked.

"How about you go home and make the batch for tomorrow; I think Dante and I will do all right here."

"Sounds good. I'll make extras for us." Candice gave her a quick smile and left, letting the door swing shut behind her. A moment later, it opened again. A woman a few years younger than Moira strode in. She was wearing dark boots and a long black coat, and her red hair was pulled up in a tight bun on the top of her head. It was evident by the way she was dressed that she wasn't from the town; most likely she was a tourist here for the Winter Festival.

"Hello, and welcome to Darling's DELIcious Delights," the deli owner greeted her. "How can I help you?"

"Are you the owner?" the woman asked.

"Yes, I am. Moira Darling." She extended her hand, and the other woman gave it a brisk shake.

"Denise Donovan," she replied. "I'm the owner of the Redwood Grill—the new restaurant in town. You may have heard of us."

"I have, actually," Moira said. "It's nice to meet you. I didn't know your restaurant was open yet. I'll have to stop by sometime."

"Our grand opening is tonight. Feel free to come if you'd like. I'm expecting it to be busy. We've been working hard to get everything ready for the first night of the Winter Festival."

"I'll see if my daughter wants to go there for dinner with me after we close. I'll go even if she doesn't want to, though." She smiled at the other woman. "It's nice to see another businesswoman. If you don't mind me asking, where are you from?"

"I was born in California, but moved to Michigan when I got married. This is the second restaurant in the chain; my husband runs the other one. He's in town right now to help out with opening night, though." She returned Moira's smile, the sharp lines of her face softening for a moment. "Thank you for your kind words. I have to admit, I wasn't expecting you to be so friendly. The man who owns that diner didn't seem very happy that another restaurant was opening up in town."

"Arlo's just grumpy, he'll come around," Moira assured her. "And I think our restaurants are different enough that there won't be much of a problem. Plus, we women have got to stick together." The two business owners traded another quick smile before Denise left to finish preparing for her grand opening. Moira watched her go, feeling happier than she had since her strange encounter with the man that morning. It seemed that she had just made another friend.

After closing the deli for the evening, she made a quick stop at home to change and see if Candice wanted to go to the Redwood Grill with her. The house was warm from all of the baking that her daughter had been doing, and the air smelled like cookies. She was amazed to see plate after plate of sugar cookies when she walked into the kitchen; Candice really had been busy.

It only took a few moments for her daughter to agree to go with her to the new restaurant. Moira waited in the kitchen while the young woman changed, and was unable to resist eating one of the cookies. The homemade frosting was perfect, and had dried to a crisp layer on top of the cookie itself, which was moist and full of flavor. *I'll really have to watch what I eat this week if I don't want to go up a pants size*, she thought. She had terrible willpower around desserts; it was one of the reasons that she didn't bake much.

"All right, I'm ready," Candice said, bounding into the room in a rush of perfume and sleek blonde hair. Moira had suggested that they both wear something dressier than usual, and her daughter had definitely gone all out.

"Let's go," she replied, feeling her stomach growl. The cookie had been tasty, but it wasn't filling. "I'm starving."

FOUR

The Redwood Grill might have been in the same building as the Soup Shoppe, but it couldn't have looked more different. The windows were now tinted so that the diners inside had privacy, and the sign glowed a deep red in the dark winter night. Inside, the air smelled of sizzling meat and a mouth-watering mixture of spices. Moira was glad to see that the restaurant was indeed busy; people were milling around at the bar and chatting as they waited for a table, and waiters and waitresses rushed back and forth carrying trays laden with food. When Moira gave her name to the hostess, she was surprised to find that Denise had reserved a table for them.

"What do you think?" she asked her daughter as the server led them through the busy restaurant to a secluded corner booth in the back.

"It seems nice." Candice looked around, admiration evident. "It's a lot fancier than any other place in town. I think they'll do well—as long as the food is up to par, of course."

They ordered drinks from the server, and then began perusing the menu, occasionally looking up to make comments to each other about what was being offered. The Redwood Grill had steaks in every cut imaginable, but also fresh seafood, tempting pasta entrées, and a whole menu page devoted to desserts.

"Hey, Mom," her daughter whispered suddenly, her eyes shifting to the left. "Look over there. Isn't that the food critic that gave us a bad review?" Moira followed the young woman's gaze and saw the familiar curls of the man who had refused to finish her soup.

"It's definitely him," she whispered back. "Oh dear, I hope he gives Denise a fair review. She's obviously put a lot of work into the place."

"I'm sure he will," her daughter replied. "Everything here looks and smells delicious. He'd be crazy to try to give this place a bad review. I can't wait to try something—I just can't decide what."

A few minutes after their food appeared and they had had a chance to taste each of the dishes that they had ordered—each one seeming better than the next—a handsome man who looked to be about Moira's age appeared at the table. He was finely dressed, with a sharp black suit, a silk tie, and shoes that looked like they cost more than Moira's car. There was a red rose tucked into his lapel, which he straightened before speaking.

"Johan Donovan," he said by way of introduction. "I hope our food is satisfactory. My wife tells me that you are quite the chef yourself." His dark brown eyes met Moira's as he said this, and to her embarrassment she felt a flush rise on her cheeks. The wine must be going to her head—this man was obviously Denise's husband, and thus completely unavailable.

"Everything was delicious," she assured him. "The steak was cooked perfectly, not overdone like it seems to be at most restaurants, and the potatoes were creamy and practically melted in my mouth."

"You've definitely won us over," Candice chimed in. "I don't know how I'm going to stay away from this place."

"No need to stay away," Johan said with a smile. "We're open every evening, and welcome your company." He took Moira's hand, and, to her surprise, kissed the back of it. "It was a pleasure to meet you, Ms. Darling. If you ever need anything, don't hesitate to call. We restaurateurs have to stick together." He slipped a business card out of his pocket and put it on the table, then released her hand. "I'll have someone bring you a dessert menu —you *must* try the lava cake, it's our chef's specialty on the house, of course." He gave them a wink, just as the tall, red-headed form of Denise appeared at his shoulder.

"Johan," she said sharply. "One of the busboys just quit, and the sous chef is having a mental break-down. I need you in back of the house, *dealing* with things. I thought we were past all this?" She arched her eyebrow, giving Moira an icy look. Confused, the deli owner looked away, pretending to focus on her food in an effort to give the pair privacy for what was obviously a personal conversation.

"I was just saying hi to your new friend, dear," he said. "It's best to stay on good terms with the competition, don't you agree? I'll go take care of the sous chef now, don't you worry." With that, he drifted off, weaving his way around busy servers and bustling customers with ease.

"My husband," Denise said simply, looking after him with an unreadable expression. She turned back to Moira, none of her earlier friendliness visible. "I just came by to see how you are doing, but it looks like he beat me to it. I hope the two of you have a good night, and *do* try the lava cake." A humorless smile twisted her lips. "It's to die for."

It was late by the time the two women got home. Both of them had eaten far too much at the restaurant, but the juicy steaks had been worth it. The lava cake had been amazing as well, though she would have enjoyed it more if she hadn't been trying to figure out what had happened between her and Denise. She had thought that the two of them had hit it off when they spoke at the deli. Maybe Denise had just been stressed at the grill tonight—logical, as it was the grand opening. Either way, the Redwood Grill had just become a new favorite for both her and Candice, though they would have to restrain themselves to eating there just once or twice a month. The food wasn't cheap, and the portions weren't small, bad for both her wallet and her waistline.

Full and groggy, she managed to drag herself upstairs and change into her pajamas before she collapsed into bed. It had been a fun evening, and she was beginning to look forward to the rest of the week, even though it would be busy. The Winter Festival marked the last long stretch of winter before spring came, and she was looking forward to all of the opportunities of the year ahead.

FIVE

The second day of the Winter Festival was in full swing as she drove into town that morning. Banners hung from windows, announcing the week's sales, and snowflakes and Valentine's hearts seemed to be everywhere she looked. The small bed and breakfast on Main Street had a full parking lot, and there were plenty of pedestrians traveling to-and-fro on the sidewalk. It was turning out to be a busy week, which Moira welcomed. She was more than happy to help Candice with her dream of opening a candy shop, but the money had to come from somewhere.

She was humming to herself as she unlocked the deli's front door, eager to get started on the day's soups—curried corn chowder, and green bean minestrone. She had never made the corn chowder before, but the recipe looked simple and delicious. After wiping her shoes off on the rug, she made her way to the cash register to unlock it and make sure they had enough one-dollar bills for the day. A shadowy form in the corner caught her eye, and she looked up, choking back a scream when she saw a man sitting at the corner table.

He was sitting slouched in the bistro chair, head drooping towards his chest. The brown curls of his hair looked familiar to Moira, but her panicked mind couldn't place them. He was wearing a brown suit, and had a red rose tucked into his lapel pocket. What was he *doing* here? He looked like he was passed out. Was it possible that some drunk had wandered in late last night? No... the front door had definitely been locked when she got here, and she only used the side door for deliveries—it locked automatically when it was shut.

"Excuse me?" she said hesitantly when the man didn't respond to her strangled yelp. He still didn't move. Cautiously, she approached, gripping her keys in her hand tightly as protection.

"Sir... are you all right?" It wasn't until she was a few feet away that she noticed the dark stain down the front of his jacket and the red smear on his hand. Her heart pounded, but unable to stop herself, she gently tilted the man's head back to find herself gazing into blank, staring eyes.

———

She was in a state of shock as she watched the crime scene photographers snap picture after picture of her deli. The front door had been propped open, letting in the icy air. Salt and snow had been tracked across the usually clean floor of the deli, and the parking lot was full of emergency vehicles.

"Do you know the victim?" the taciturn Detective Fitzgerald asked her, his pen poised and ready against his notepad.

"I, um..." She found her gaze dragged once again towards the man in the chair, his body half obscured by one of the crime scene technicians. "Yes. He's a food critic. He comes here every year for the Winter Festival."

"Do you know his name?"

"Jason Platte," she said.

"Thank you, ma'am, that will be helpful. He doesn't have ID on him." The detective sighed and rubbed his eyes; he looked older than he had when Moira had met him only a few months ago. "I think that's everything I need from you right now. We'll be in contact, I'm sure. You can either wait here, or get going home; this will probably take most of the day."

"I'll leave—I need to tell my daughter what happened, and I really don't want to have to see any more of this than I have to." She hesitated, reluctant to leave her store alone even with the police. "Do you think you could have someone call me when you're done? I just want to stop by and make sure everything is locked up."

"Sure." Fitzgerald made a note on his pad before snapping it shut and putting it in his pocket. "I'll have someone give you a call when we're done. You know the drill: the deli is closed, but you need to stick around and be prepared to come down to the station if we need you to answer any more questions." Moira nodded, and then grabbed her purse and numbly made for the door. She didn't know what she would tell Candice, or how long the shop would be closed for. She just knew that once again, a tragic crime had struck too close to her life.

She walked into a house redolent of cookies and peppermint. She had forgotten that Candice had been planning on bringing in another batch of cookies when she came in to work—she was just glad that *she* had opened the store today, not her daughter or either of her other employees. Finding the food critic had been horrible, but it would have been a hundred times worse if her daughter had been the one to find him.

"Hi, sweetie," Moira said, poking her head into the kitchen to see her daughter dressed in an apron with flour everywhere. The peppermint smell was even stronger.

"Mom, what are you doing here? I thought you were opening the store this morning." She saw the look on her mother's face and immediately quit rolling out the dough that she had been working on. "What happened?"

"Someone died." Moira took a deep breath, and then began telling her daughter what had happened to her that morning.

PATTI BENNING

"Wow, I can't believe it. Do you think it was an accident?" Her daughter peered at a candy thermometer that was poking out of a pot on the stove, then shook her head and turned her attention back to her mother.

"An accident? No, I don't see how it could be. I mean, he was bleeding from some sort of wound." Moira shook her head. "I don't think he would stab himself or whatever happened, and then decide to just sit down and wait while he bled out."

"I guess." Candice shuddered. "That means that someone else did it, though. Someone killed a guy in your deli." Her daughter looked pale, and Moira reached an arm out to steady her.

"I'm sure the police will figure things out soon." She found herself wishing vehemently that she had installed security cameras like David had suggested when she had first met him.

"Do you think they'll blame you? I mean, he did give the deli a bad review, and he was killed in a building you own…"

"They didn't seem very suspicious," she said, thinking back over the conversation. "But I guess they might think I had something to do with it." She sighed. "I'll just do what I did last time I was a suspect... be honest, and do what I can to help."

"And call David?" her daughter asked, giving her a weak grin.

"Maybe." Moira couldn't help but to smile to herself at the thought of the handsome private investigator. "What are you making?" she asked with a nod towards the pot on the stove in an effort to distract her daughter.

"Oh, I'm just trying to make some peppermint hard candies. It's a pretty simple recipe, so I thought it would be a good one to start out with." She eyed the thermometer once again, and then sighed. "It's just a pain waiting for it to get up to the perfect temperature, and I have to keep stirring so it doesn't burn."

"It smells amazing; if they turn out well, you can sell them alongside the cookies when we reopen." She sighed, her thoughts brought back to the dead man in the deli. "I think I'm going to head upstairs for a bit. Let me know when the candies are done; I definitely want to try one."

Deciding that she should be comfortable since she couldn't work, Moira threw on a pair of sweatpants and a loose tee shirt, then collapsed into bed. She still felt emotionally numb; after the shock of seeing the dead food critic, it was hard to feel anything else. It was terrible that he was dead, there was no denying that. But what she was beginning to feel more than sadness, was fear. Fear for herself, for her daughter, and even for her business. Someone had been in her store. Someone had *killed* Jason Platte in her store and left him there. It felt personal, and that was terrifying.

She considered her options. Of course the police would investigate, but what was she supposed to do until they caught the killer? Could she really be comfortable in the deli knowing that someone had been murdered there? And how had Jason Platte and his killer even gotten in? There were too many questions for her to answer by herself. She was reluctant to turn to David for help so soon; he would start to think that she attracted trouble. Unable to sleep, she lay in bed until her daughter's voice called up the stairs, letting her know that the peppermint candies were done and ready to be tested.

SIX

"This was a good idea," Moira told her daughter, giving her a quick smile before turning her attention back to the road. "Getting out of the house was probably the best thing I could do. Otherwise I'd just be lying in bed, thinking about what happened and waiting for the police to call."

"Thanks for coming with me. I know it's a bit early to start looking, but I just want to see what's available," Candice replied. She offered her mother another peppermint candy, dusted with powdered sugar and wrapped in wax paper. They had turned out well, sweet and minty without being overwhelming.

"It's exciting, isn't it?" she asked as she took the candy. It was a bittersweet trip that they were taking.

She and her daughter were going to drive around Lake Marion, Maple Creek's neighboring town, and look at apartments and small commercial spaces. They wouldn't be able to actually rent a place until the tourist season picked up, but it would give them both a good feel of what to expect.

Candice had only ever been out of the house for the time that she had spent at college getting her associate's degree. Moira knew that it was reasonable to expect her daughter to move out at some point, but it was still an emotional event. They had finally developed a good relationship and she didn't want to lose that. As a teen, Candice had blamed Moira for her parents' divorce. It hadn't been until her daughter had returned from college that they had finally begun to communicate and work together. Now, the young woman was a trusted and valuable part of the deli, as well as a caring and responsible daughter.

"I'm going to miss you," she added, popping the candy into her mouth.

"I know, Mom. I'm going to miss you too. But I won't be far away, and I'll visit you whenever I can."

"No, no, you should feel free to live your own life. Don't worry about me." She slowed the car as they pulled into the city limits. The lake that gave the small town its name was a white expanse of ice to their right. A few huts for ice fishing were set up on it, and there was one man trudging carefully towards one. "It's a nice town, and I'm sure you'll feel right at home pretty quickly."

They began their search on Main Street, cruising slowly along and making note of the few *For Lease* and *For Sale* signs that they saw. They knew that a central location would be best. They needed the perfect location so that plenty of drivers could see the store, as well as an area where there would be a lot of foot traffic. The only problem was, nothing good seemed to be for lease. The only suitably sized building that they found was far down a side street.

"Well... maybe some places will open up in the summer," Candice said with a disappointed sigh. "That corner building would be perfect for me."

"You never know; anything might happen." She gave her daughter a reassuring smile. "Things will work out. Now, how about some coffee before we head home?"

David Morris tapped his fingers slowly on his thigh as he stared at the papers spread out in front of him. No matter how hard he stared, the words seemed to swim away from his tired eyes. It wasn't even that late, but darkness was falling, and the coffee in the paper cup on the table was getting cold. Pretty soon, he would either have to order another cup, or leave.

When the door to the small coffee shop jingled open, he looked up automatically. He did a double take when he saw who it was. The cute deli owner who seemed to attract trouble like a magnet was walking in with her daughter like she owned the place. *What business could they have in Lake Marion?* he wondered.

"Moira," he called out, half rising from his seat to catch her attention.

"David!" she exclaimed, once her eyes found him. He forced himself not to show how pleased he was when she smiled at him. He'd never gotten the feeling that she reciprocated his feelings and he wasn't about to push it.

"What brings you here?" he asked, clearing the table so that she and her daughter could sit with him. He dumped the papers unceremoniously into the bag ; he could get back to work tomorrow.

"Oh, we were just looking around at storefronts." She gave a small laugh and wrinkled her nose. "Nothing good is available though. Say... you wouldn't know of any businesses that are going under, would you?"

"Why, are you relocating?" he asked hopefully. If she opened up a deli here, chances were he would stop by every day for soup and a sandwich.

"It's for Candice," she replied. "She's going to be opening her own shop in Lake Marion—a candy shop, with all homemade candies. She just tried out a peppermint hard candy recipe that turned out very well."

"Here, I actually have one left. You can have it." The daughter reached into her purse and pulled out a small candy wrapped in wax paper, which he took. "I'm going to go order our coffee, I'll be right back."

"So, what's new in your life?" David asked as Candice walked away. "Business going well?'

"Yes, it is, thankfully. Except—" She hesitated, biting her lip and looking at him regretfully. "Ah... someone was murdered in the deli this morning."

"Are you serious?" He stared at her uncertainly. It didn't seem like the kind of joke that she would play, but he just couldn't believe that she was involved in yet another murder, and this one so close to home.

"I am," she sighed. "It was horrible. I found him this morning and... I knew him." She took a deep breath and sat down, burying her head in her hands. "I saw him just yesterday, at a new restaurant, and he was fine. And then today..." She trailed off, and David reached out to pat her arm. He didn't know what to say. Moira had been through more than a lot of people that he knew. She was strong in many ways, but there was only so much that one person could deal with.

"I'm sorry," he said. "Did you know him well?"

"No, I'd only met him once before, actually." She choked out a short laugh. "He was a food critic, and gave my deli a bad review last year. I'm sure once the police find that out, they'll be all over me."

"Do you know how he died?" It was David's nature to seek answers even to difficult questions, which was one of the reasons that he had been able to make a living as a private investigator. It wasn't so bad to work all the time if you loved your job.

"Not really. But there was a bloodstain on the front of his shirt. I think he might have been stabbed," she told him. A quick glance around reassured her that Candice wasn't back yet, so she continued. "He was just sitting in the chair, kind of slouched down, like someone had propped him up." She imitated the corpse's positioning. "I just can't get over the fact that someone was in the deli, someone who killed a guy, and they could come back at any time."

"You really need security cameras. Or at least some sort of alarm system," he pointed out. He paused, considering his next words carefully. He didn't want to scare her, but he did want to let her know just how serious the situation was. "You should have something that will alert you if the doors are opened during the night. Right now, someone could break in when the deli is closed and hide out in the kitchen, and you wouldn't know until it was too late."

"Don't say that." She shivered. "I already feel like I'll never be comfortable again."

"Sorry," he said. "I just don't want to see you get hurt... or worse."

Candice returned at that moment, and conversation turned to her plans for the future. Before the two women left, he promised to stop by within the next few days to help her install some sort of security. He hated the thought of her involved with yet another crime, but he knew that there wasn't anything he could do to keep her out of trouble; she had a nose for it.

Moira got the all clear from Detective Jefferson on her drive back to Maple Creek, so the next morning she arrived at the deli even earlier than usual to clean up. She had been unable to get David's words out of her head the entire night before, so she did a quick but thorough search of the kitchen to reassure herself that no one was hiding and ready to jump out at her.

To her relief, there was no sign that a dead man had been sitting in the chair a day before, though the floor was a mess from all of the salt and snow that had been tracked in and melted. It took her nearly two hours to clean up, but when she was done, the deli was sparkling.

Once the deli was back to normal, she breathed a sigh of relief and began pulling out the pots and pans that she would need to make the soups. She didn't know how many customers she should be expecting today; last time someone's death had been connected to the store, business had suffered terribly until she had cleared her name. Hopefully it wouldn't be the same this time.

She began by melting a stick of butter in a large Dutch oven, then she added sliced leeks, celery, and carrots. While the vegetables softened in the butter on low heat, she got started on the minestrone. Soon enough, the scents of garlic browning in olive oil and sizzling butter filled the kitchen. Deciding to make the most of her early morning, she turned on the radio and soon found herself humming along as she worked. The deli was *hers* and she refused to be scared while she was there. The front door was locked, and she had checked every nook and cranny of the kitchen; there was nothing to worry about.

A blast of cold air made her spin around, and a jolt of adrenaline shot through her when she saw the side door that they used for deliveries open, and a tall man with a dark coat standing in its entrance, silhouetted against the bright sunlight outside. It took her eyes a moment to adjust to the contrast, but when she recognized David's blue eyes and amused expression, she let out a huge sigh and put down the spoon that she had been holding in front of her like a sword.

"You scared me half to death," she said.

"Sorry. I didn't mean to." He let himself the rest of the way in, and shut the door behind him. "I tried knocking at the front door, but you weren't answering, so I thought I would try back here."

"I was listening to music." Embarrassed, Moira turned the radio down. "But how did you get in? That door is always locked. It locks automatically. I have to prop it open."

"It wasn't locked this time," he said with a frown. He pulled the door partway open again and crouched down. She watched as he slowly peeled a piece of tape away from the latch. Their eyes met, and she felt a shiver go down her spine. Someone had kept the door from locking, and had had access to the deli for who knew how long without her having a clue.

"Oh, my goodness," she said, sitting down on one of the tall stools and staring at David. "Should I tell the police?"

"Definitely," he said. "Do you have a sandwich bag?"

Confused, she stood up and got the container of plastic bags from the cupboard. She handed him one, and watched as he carefully put the piece of tape, that had been holding the latch down, inside of it.

I don't want to contaminate it, in case they can use it as evidence," he told her. "They may be able to lift fingerprints from it."

"Oh, that makes sense. Can you stir the soups? They're simmering, I just don't want them to burn." She grabbed her cell phone. "I'm going to call Detective Jefferson and tell him what we found."

When she came back into the kitchen, she was amused to find the private investigator carefully stirring the curried corn chowder. He was peering at the soup doubtfully, as if he wasn't quite certain what it was supposed to be.

"What are you doing here, anyway?" she asked, taking the spoon from him and giving the soup a quick stir before moving on to check on the minestrone.

"Oh, I came over to help you install a couple of things that I picked up—if you want them, of course," he said.

"Like what?" She raised her eyebrows, surprised by his thoughtfulness.

"There's a motion detector and a wireless security camera that you can access from your phone," he told her. "They're yours if you want them. I figure that with everything that has been going on here, you'd appreciate a little added security."

"I do appreciate it, but you didn't have to do all of that for me. I was planning on getting something. Eventually." She sighed, knowing that she would have kept putting it off. She was okay with technology, but she thought that choosing which security camera to go with and installing it would probably be beyond her.

"They're nothing fancy," he said quickly. "I just thought it might help."

"Thank you." She gave him a quick smile. "Oh, Detective Jefferson and Detective Fitzgerald are going to stop by. They said they want to pick up the tape, and also talk to me. You can stay though, if you want," she added quickly.

"All right, I'll get started on installing the camera and motion detector if you want. Just tell me where to put them."

SEVEN

The detectives arrived only a few minutes after David began to install the security camera. Moira had opted to put it up front by the register, as she had seen many stores do. She figured that if the deli was ever robbed or there were any problems with a customer, it would all be on film. She thought it was neat that she would be able to check in through her phone even when she wasn't there, though she hoped that her employees wouldn't feel like she was spying on them. She trusted them completely, she just needed to do what was necessary to feel safe. The motion detector she decided to put in the kitchen, where it would pick up the movement of anyone coming in the door. It would send an alert to her phone if it detected motion during the hours that the deli was closed.

"Hello, Ms. Darling. Thanks for calling us," said Detective Jefferson when she unlocked the front door for him. The deli was supposed to open in less than an hour, and she sincerely hoped that the police business would be finished by then. He gave David a nod, and then turned his attention back to her.

"Here's the tape we found." She handed him the bag. "I don't know how long it was on there. I hate to say it, but I never really checked to see if the door was locked. I just assumed it was, and we only use it for deliveries, so it could have gone unnoticed for a long time."

"If it's okay, Detective Fitzgerald would like to take a look around. While he does that, do you mind if I ask you some questions?" he asked. She nodded and followed the detective over to one of the small tables while his partner slipped into the kitchen.

"We've been looking into the murder victim's past, to see who might have a motive," he told her. "And we found his review of your deli. It was pretty bad."

"Yeah." Moira grimaced. "It was totally unfair. He was rude the entire time, and ended up throwing out most of his meal. I know Darling's DELIcious Delights isn't a five-star, award-winning sort of place, but we do have good food, good employees, and a nice atmosphere. All of which he basically said were terrible."

"So, is it safe to say that you disliked Jason Platte?" he asked.

"Well..." She frowned, trying to choose her words carefully so that they would be honest, but wouldn't sound like she was still unduly upset with the man. He had died in the deli, after all. She must at least be a person of interest in the case. "I don't like the way he treated me or my employees, and I don't like that he barely even gave my food a chance," she began, "but I didn't know him personally. For all I know, he might have just had a really bad day. His review didn't really affect the deli much, anyway. My regulars are smart enough not to listen to him, and most of the tourists just kind of stop in when they're driving through; they don't bother to look up reviews." The detective nodded and leaned back in his chair.

"Do you have any idea who put the tape on your door so it wouldn't lock shut?" he asked.

"I don't have a clue," she told him honestly. "The employees all have keys, and we don't allow customers in the back. Someone could have snuck back there and done it, I guess. Or maybe one of the delivery guys did it, but I really don't see why they would."

"Has anything gone missing lately? Even things too small for you to bother reporting, like food, or small appliances."

"Nothing that I can think of," she said. "Why? Do you think someone has been stealing from us?"

"Possibly. If an unknown person had access to your store, they could have been doing anything," he pointed out.

"It's bad enough that someone was killed here; the fact that some creepy killer has had a way into my store for who knows how long makes it even worse." She shuddered. "I don't know if I'll ever feel completely comfortable here again."

"Actually..." Jefferson darted his gaze towards the back to make sure that David wasn't listening in, and then he leaned towards Moira and lowered his voice. "The victim wasn't killed here; he was killed elsewhere and then moved here. I don't know if that makes you feel any better, but at least your restaurant wasn't the scene of a murder."

"Thanks for telling me," she said. "Last night, I kept imagining what must have happened. It was terrible. I barely slept."

A moment later, Fitzgerald came back out of the kitchen and nodded to David, who was standing on a step stool, marking where the screws for the security camera would go. He turned to where his partner sat with Moira.

"You all set?" he asked.

"For now." The younger detective rose and extended a hand to Moira, which she shook. "Thank you for your time, and please let us know if you find anything else that may be evidence."

"Of course," she said. "Thanks for responding so quickly. I hope you catch the killer soon."

To her surprise, people began lining up outside the deli before they even opened. Candice was supposed to come in later, but Moira was beginning to wish that she had asked her to open with her today. Luckily, David was there, and once he had finished installing the camera and motion detector, he helped out by bringing bowls of soup out of the kitchen for her. Towards the end of the lunch rush, a familiar face appeared in the crowd.

"Hi, Steven, wasn't it?" she asked. The man nodded. "How can I help you today?"

"I'll, um, have a bowl of the curried corn chowder," he said. "And I just wanted to say, the invitation is still open... you know, for the dance."

"Thank you," she said, "but I don't think I'll change my mind about going. Dances aren't really my thing." She accepted the crumpled bills that he gave her and told David, who had just appeared from the kitchen, what the new order was. After handing Steven his change, she wondered what else she could say. He set her on edge and she couldn't decide why. It might just have been that he was the first man to ask her out in a long time.

"Soup's up," David said, coming back out of the kitchen and handing her the to-go bowl of soup, which she deftly put in a paper bag and then handed to the man. Or, she attempted to. He was staring at David with an odd, tense look on his face.

"Here's your order," she said, clearing her throat. He blinked and reached out for it, then left without another word.

Once the lunch rush was over, Moira ladled some soup into bowls for her and David, and sat down with him at a table. She was thankful for the business, but the morning had been stressful. Most customers had been more interested in ogling the corner where the food critic had been found, and asking her about what had happened, than they were in what they were buying. Though she had been polite and friendly, she was glad that the rush was over—for now. The last thing she wanted was to spend the entire day talking about finding a dead man in her store.

"Thanks for helping out so much," she told him. "You didn't need to."

"It was my pleasure. I never realized how much work it is to manage this place."

"Well, it's usually not this bad. And I've got backup coming in soon," she said. "So, can you show me how to use the security camera and the motion detector? Candice is the one that's good at this stuff, not me."

"Sure. Give me your phone."

As David installed the app that went with the security camera, Moira began cleaning up their dishes and tidying the shelves, which always seemed to get messy faster than she thought possible. The front door opened, and she looked around, ready to jump behind the counter again for another customer. Instead, she saw her daughter with a platter of cookies balanced with one hand and a newspaper rolled up in the other.

"Hey, Mom," she said. "Can you take this? There's another plate in the car."

"Sure. Those look delicious; I might have to try one or two before we sell any."

Once the cookies were in and set safely on the counter, Candice greeted David, and then pulled a third chair up to the small table.

"Did you guys see this?" she asked, unrolling the newspaper and turning it so both he and Moira could see it. The two of them peered at the article for a moment, reading it silently while Candice tapped her foot impatiently.

"Interesting," David said when he had finished. He leaned back in his chair and drummed his fingers on the table.

"And we did see him there the night before he died, remember, Mom?" Candice asked eagerly.

"That's true..." Moira frowned at the paper. The article was a special edition restaurant review, written by Jason Platte the night before he had been found dead in the deli. The review was for the Redwood Grill, and it was almost as bad as the review that he had submitted about Darling's DELI-cious Delights. "But you don't really think that someone from that restaurant could have killed him, do you?" she asked, looking at her daughter.

"Well, maybe. If your friend Denise knew he was writing such a bad review of her restaurant's opening night, who knows what she could have done," she pointed out.

"But why would she take his body here?" The deli owner frowned, not willing to be convinced that Denise had anything to do with the murder. After all, *she* had gotten a bad review, and she hadn't killed anyone.

"I'm not saying I think she's the killer," David cut in. "But as for why she would have deposited the body here, well... you *are* competition. If she made it look like you had killed him, she would have been getting rid of two birds with one stone."

"Nonsense. Our restaurants aren't anything alike. If someone wants a steak, they'll go to the Redwood Grill. If they want soup or cheese or cold cuts, they'll come here." She sighed. "She just met me, for goodness sake. She reserved me a table at the grill. She just doesn't seem like a killer to me." David raised his eyebrows, and Moira remembered that her recent track record of reading people was iffy at best.

"I just thought it was a weird coincidence." Her daughter shrugged. "I'm sure the police will find whoever it is. So, Mom, did you install security cameras?" she asked, changing the subject.

"David installed them for me," she told her daughter, shooting a grateful smile at the private investigator. "There's the camera up front, and a motion detector in the back."

"Which reminds me, I've got to show you how to use the app before I go." He explained the process, and watched in amusement for a moment as she and Candice played around with the new technology, then he let himself out the door and headed towards his car. He had work to do.

EIGHT

As soon as people started getting out of work, the dinner rush began, and Moira and Candice were kept busy right up until close. Just as she was about to turn the deadbolt on the front door, a car pulled into the parking lot. She sighed and pulled back. One more customer wouldn't hurt, and she always hated to turn away someone who had made a special trip just to get something from the deli.

She was surprised to see Johan Donovan get out of the car, dressed nearly as nicely as he had been on the opening night of his wife's restaurant. Suddenly feeling self-conscious, she glanced around the deli, noting a napkin on the floor, the disorganized array of cheeses that she hadn't had time to fix, and the smudges on one of the windows of the glass display case left by an unruly child. The Redwood Grill had been so perfect; what would he think of her restaurant?

"Hello," he said, pausing at the door. "I was just driving by, and thought I would see how you were doing."

"Very well, thank you," she said, something about the casual way he leaned against the doorframe putting her on edge. She smelled the faint scent of liquor on him, and realized that he must have just come from the bar. "We were actually just about to close," she said. "Can I get you anything?"

"No, I just wanted to see your pretty face again." He leered at her, raising a hand as if to brush her hair aside, but thinking better of it when she stepped away from his touch.

"Do you need me to call you a cab, Mr. Donovan?" she said, feeling more uncomfortable by the minute. The man was married—he shouldn't be acting like this.

"Call me Johan." He grinned at her. "And no, I'll be fine. Your concern is touching."

"I know Denise would be heartbroken if something happened to you," she said pointedly. "Please be careful on the roads, once you get out of town, they're pretty bad." She glanced back, pretending to check the clock. "And if you're sure you don't need a cab, I really should be closing. It's been a long day."

"Oh, you're no fun." He teased, huffing out a sigh. "But if you insist, I'll go home, to my *wife*, and get out of your hair. Call me if you decide you want to have some fun." He winked, then turned and weaved his way back to his car.

Relieved, Moira watched as he started the vehicle and exited the parking lot. She firmly turned the deadbolt on the door, glad that he was out of her hair. Some men were just creeps; she felt bad for Denise, who was stuck with him. The encounter at the restaurant made sense now; it was obvious that the other woman knew at least something of her husband's disloyalty.

***

She was so preoccupied with her thoughts of Johan and Denise that it wasn't until the two of them got home and settled down at the table that she realized

Candice had been unusually quiet, her attention taken up by the glowing screen of the cell phone in her hand.

"Something going on?" she asked.

"Um, no," her daughter put her phone down, blushing. "Not really. Sorry; I'll keep it off while we eat."

"You know you can talk to me, right, sweetheart?"

"I know," she stirred her bowl of reheated soup for a second, and then looked up with a shy smile on her face. "I have a boyfriend. I was going to tell you, but you seemed upset about everything that had happened, and it just didn't seem like the right time."

"That's great news. Is he taking you to the dance?"

"Yeah. I thought I might go shopping for a dress tomorrow, once I'm done with the day's batch of cookies. They shouldn't take too long; I've already got the dough chilling in the fridge."

"I'm happy for you. If you need help with anything, let me know. I'll take the last shift at the deli before the dance by myself, so you'll have time to get ready,"

Moira said, beaming at her daughter. "When can I meet him?

"Thanks, Mom." Candice grinned back. "And I guess I can stop by the deli with him sometime. He wanted to see it anyway."

"Bring him in for lunch or dinner sometime, on me."

"I definitely will. I think you'll like him." The young woman took a bite of her soup, and then added, "You should get a boyfriend. Or at least go on some dates."

"I'll think about it," she said. Maybe she *should* date. After all, she needed more in her life than just the deli, didn't she?

NINE

The next day was just as busy, but luckily both Darrin and Dante were available to help her out. She hid in the back for the most part, not wanting to hear the gossip or have to watch the strange, morbid fascination with which people examined the table where Jason Platte had been found. When Darrin came back to the kitchen to tell her that someone was asking for her, she reluctantly agreed to go and speak with them. She had been half expecting to see Steven, the man who kept asking her to the dance, but instead was surprised to see a good-looking man with lush blonde hair that was just starting to gray around the edges. His pale blue eyes sparkled when he saw her.

"Moira Darling?" he asked with a very slight Russian accent.

"Yes," she said, somewhat warily. She didn't see any cameras or microphones, but he could be a reporter. She had had a few of those come around, but asked them to leave almost immediately.

"I'm Marcus Noskov. I think Martha Washburn told you about me?"

"She did." Moira shook his hand, using the moment to look at him again with new eyes. So, *this* was Martha's boyfriend's cousin? He was definitely good looking. So good looking, in fact, that she had to wonder why he would be interested in her.

"I just moved to the next town over, and everyone there is talking about Maple Creek's Winter Festival," he said. "If it's not too late to ask, I'd love to take you to the dance this Sunday. Martha has told me so much about you and what you did to help her and her sister. I was thinking, if you accept my invitation, we might go with them as a sort of double date. We can all go out to dinner first at that new grill."

"Oh, um..." She hadn't dated in a long time, and hadn't gone to the Valentine's dance in City Hall for even longer. The event was part fundraiser, part tradition. There would be a raffle, music, and some snacks and drinks if this year was anything like the previous ones. It *would* be fun to go, and if she went with Marcus, Martha, and the man that Martha was seeing, it wouldn't be as serious a date as if she and Marcus were going strictly as a pair.

"That actually sounds really nice," she said. "I won't be able to do dinner, since I just told my daughter that I would close here that night, but I would love to accept your invitation to the dance."

"Great," he said with a grin that revealed perfectly white teeth. "I'll pick you up at seven?"

"Sure." They traded numbers, and chatted a little bit more until customers began to line up behind him. Moira spent the next half hour ringing up orders with a smile on her face. Somehow, the constant questions and conversations about the food critic's death didn't seem to bother her quite as much anymore.

Candice stopped in shortly after to refresh their supply of cookies. She had a young man in tow; he looked to be a few years older than her. He wore his red hair pulled back into a ponytail, which Moira might have found worrying if she hadn't noticed the utter adoration in his eyes as he looked at her daughter.

"Mom, this is Adrian Cook, the guy I was telling you about." She set down the tray of cookies, and indicated for Adrian to do the same. "He offered to help me with the cookies this morning, and I thought it would be a good chance for you to meet him."

"Nice to meet you," Moira said.

"You too, Ms. Darling," he replied, shaking her hand.

"Thanks for bringing the cookies—we were almost out." She moved the last few cookies from the old tray to the new one, and then handed the old tray off to Darrin to be washed and dried. She would take it home tonight to use for the cookies tomorrow. "So, how did you two meet?"

"We went to college together and stayed in contact online." Her daughter turned to smile at her boyfriend. "He's interested in business, too, so we're going to Lake Marion tomorrow to look around some more and maybe talk to some people about my plans for opening a candy shop."

"That's great. I'm glad you have someone to help you with all of that." She nodded at Adrian. "It was nice to meet you. Like I told Candice, you two are welcome to stop by the deli for lunch or dinner sometime on me."

"Thanks, we definitely will," he said. "And it was nice to meet you, too."

"We've got to run now, Mom. I still have to buy a dress, and he's got to get to work."

Moira bid her goodbye and watched them leave, with a smile on her face and a glad heart. Maybe there was something to this whole Valentine's thing after all.

TEN

David pulled into his office later that day, his mind on things other than work. He was thinking about Moira, who always seemed to attract trouble through no fault of her own. They had developed a close friendship, but he was beginning to want something more.

They were both single and roughly the same age, so they were naturally drawn together, but was what he felt for her more than just friendship and the knowledge that smart, attractive, single women of the right age weren't exactly a dime a dozen? And if she felt anything for him, was it just convenience, or did she really like him? David wasn't a shallow person, and he didn't want anything more than friendship unless the feelings were real and deep on both sides. Unable to make up his mind about anything, he got out of the car and made his way to the office door. No matter how distracted he was, he still had to work.

He dropped his keys as he was trying to unlock the office door. Sighing, he bent down to pick them up out of the snow when, out of the corner of his eye, he saw a shadowy figure rush around the corner of the building. He just had just straightened up when something hard smashed into the back of his head. Grunting, his head exploding with pain, he fell to his knees. His assailant stepped into his line of sight, but all he saw was the ski mask covering the person's face, and the dark shape of a baseball bat rushing towards his face.

Heart pounding, and still dazed, he managed to roll to the side so that the bat hit his shoulder instead of his head. He kicked out and was able to catch the assailant on one of his shins and was rewarded with a sharp kick to his ribcage and another to his stomach. The last thing he heard before he blacked out were panicked shouts and the sound of feet rushing towards him.

ELEVEN

"So, what do you think of him, Mom, really?" Candice asked. They were frosting cookies together in the kitchen after work, so that they would have fewer to frost the next day. The deli would be donating a few hundred to the Valentine's dance, which meant that they had to make even more than usual.

"He seems nice, but I haven't really had a chance to get to know him, sweetie," Moira pointed out. "If you like him and think he's a good man, that's good enough for me."

"I do like him, and he's passionate about the same things I am," she said. "How about you? Do you actually like that Marcus guy, or did you just agree to go out with him because Martha asked you to?"

"Well, I don't know him well enough to say if I like him or not. I probably wouldn't have agreed to go to the dance with him if Martha hadn't suggested him." She sighed. "I don't have anything to wear, and I'm too old for all of this."

"It's just the same old dance that City Hall hosts every year," her daughter said. "You can wear any dress, and don't say you're too old. Half the women there will be older than you."

"And the other half will be your age," Moira pointed out. "And don't get too excited and think that this means I'm going to start dating him. It's just one outing, and we're going with Martha and the guy that she's seeing, too."

"I know, I know. I'm just glad you agreed to go. Oh, do you want to see my dress?"

"Of course." Moira set down the cookie that she had just finished frosting and looked around. When she didn't see any other unfrosted cookies, she put her knife in the sink and began cleaning up. "I'll finish here, and you go change into it. Deal?"

"Deal." Her daughter took off her apron and then disappeared through the doorway.

Moira was in the middle of doing the dishes when her cell phone buzzed in her pocket. Taking a moment to dry her soapy hands, she dug for the phone. Seeing David's name, she answered with a cheerful hello. Her good mood abruptly ended when his hoarse voice reached her ears.

"Moira," he rasped. "Something happened."

She listened to his description of the attack in shocked horror, grateful that he wasn't more seriously injured. Even though he didn't say anything about it being related to the murder of Jason Platte, she couldn't help but wonder if it was. The coincidence seemed too great for it to be otherwise.

"But you're okay?" she asked when he had finished.

"Not okay exactly," he said with a dry laugh. "But I'll live. They released me from the hospital half an hour ago."

"What did the police say? Will they be able to catch the person who did this?"

"I'm not sure. I didn't really give them a lot to go on," he replied. "They can't exactly track down every person who owns a ski mask and a baseball bat and bring them in for questioning."

"Why would someone do this to you?" she wondered.

"I've managed to make a few enemies in my time. Not everyone likes a private investigator, you know. Especially when I'm not on their side."

"Do *you* have any idea who it was?" she asked. "Did anything about the person seem familiar? It must be someone who knows you... I can't imagine why anyone would do this to a stranger."

"I didn't recognize anything about them," he said. "It was odd, though... whoever it was dropped a single red rose when they ran away."

"A red rose?" Something nagged at Moira. Where had she seen a red rose recently? She gasped suddenly. "David, the food critic had a red rose on him when I found him. It was tucked into his suit pocket, and I thought that he must have just been wearing it to dress up for some reason. But if whoever attacked you left a red rose, too..."

"Then the crimes might be connected," he finished. "Does this help you link anyone to them? Do you know any florists?"

"No, but..." she hesitated. "Well, it might not mean anything, but when Candice and I went to the Redwood Grill, we met the owner's husband, and he had a red rose tucked into his lapel. And he did come to the store to talk to me after that, which I thought was kind of odd."

"Send me any information you have on him," David said hoarsely. "I'm going to be taking it easy for a few days anyway; I might as well make myself useful by seeing what I can dig up on him."

At that moment, Candice came back into the room, wearing her new dress and carrying two different pairs of heels in her hand. When she saw her mother on the phone, she raised her eyebrows and gestured with her head back towards the kitchen door, asking if she should leave. Moira shook her head and held up a finger to get her to wait. She needed to tell her daughter what had happened.

After promising to call in the morning to check up on him, she said a hurried goodbye to David, who was going to take pain medication and go to sleep.

Then she sat down with Candice and told her what had happened—and even more chillingly, that whoever murdered Jason Platte might have also attacked David.

"Do you think whoever attacked David meant to kill him?" she asked, once Moira was done telling her what David had told her.

"I don't know. Maybe." She frowned, going over everything she knew about both crimes in her mind. She couldn't figure out what linked the murdered food critic and David. As far as she knew, they had never met. She supposed that it was possible that it was just an odd coincidence, but something in her gut told her that the same person had committed both crimes.

"I want you to be careful," she told her daughter. "We don't know what's going on, or what the motive is of whoever is behind all of this. Do you still have that pepper spray I gave you?"

"Yeah," Candice said. "I keep it in my purse."

"Make sure it's somewhere you can grab it quickly if you need to. I'll keep mine on me, too."

"I will." She got up. "I'm going to go change out of the dress—it doesn't feel right to be wearing it now. Then I think I'll go to bed. Good night, Mom."

"Good night, sweetie. I'll see you in the morning." She sat at the table for a few minutes after her daughter left, not sure if she had the energy left to finish cleaning up the kitchen. She was worried about David, and even more worried about what might happen next. She was glad that David had installed the security measures in the deli; with any luck, whoever the killer was would try to break in again and they would catch him red-handed.

TWELVE

"I'll have the Tuscan bean chili, and also this smoked cheddar and half a pound of the honey turkey breast." The woman placed a wedge of cheddar on the counter and gazed at the drink fridge. "Oh, and a bottle of that raspberry sparkling water, if that's all right. The soup's for here."

"Okay, your order will be ready in just a moment. Dante here will ring you up, and I'll go get your soup. Are you sure you don't want a sandwich with that?"

"Oh, I'd better not." The customer chuckled. "I'm watching my weight. The soup's a treat for me; it was a long day at work."

Moira ducked into the back to ladle some of the chili into a bowl. The scent of the rich vegetarian chili made her stomach grumble. It was well past lunch, and she still hadn't had a chance to eat. After this customer, she would have to leave Dante and Darrin to manage things while she took a break.

"Here you go," she said when she got back out to the register. "Enjoy, and have a nice afternoon."

"Thanks." The woman took the soup with a grateful smile and headed over to one of the corner tables to enjoy her food.

"I'm going to grab lunch really quickly," she told her two employees. "Do you think you two can handle things for a bit?"

"Sure, Ms. D.," Darrin said. "We'll come find you if we need help. I think it's starting to slow down a bit, anyway."

She settled herself down on a stool in the kitchen with a bowl of chili in front of her. The first spoonful was amazing: the fresh tomatoes were cooked to perfection and burst with flavor in her mouth, and the basil and oregano gave the unique soup some familiar flavors. She sprinkled extra parmesan cheese on top; the cheese was freshly grated and came from a local cheese maker that she knew personally. With some sparkling water to wash it down, it was the perfect meal.

When she got back out to the front, the line of customers had dwindled to just a few of her regulars, and Darrin was changing a light bulb in one of the refrigerated display cases while Dante rang someone up. As she watched her employees work, she began to realize that they were more than capable of handling the daily goings on at the deli. She really didn't need to be there as much as she was, and she was certain that the two young men and her daughter would appreciate the extra hours. Maybe she could start working one or two fewer days each week—once the Winter Festival was over, of course. That would leave her time to focus on other aspects of her life. Maybe she could get a hobby, or join some sort of local club.

The rest of the day passed slowly until five o'clock, when most people left work and the dinner rush started. Moira spent most of the time tending to some necessary minor maintenance, spackling over old nail holes in the wall and cleaning the glass in the display cases.

Once the dinner rush began, she returned to her chosen job of fetching people's orders; she preferred ladling soup and making sandwiches to hearing people talk about the food critic's death, which was still the talk of the town. It didn't help that there were more tourists than ever; as the Winter Festival progressed, more and more shops put up beautiful light displays and had special sales for charity. There was an ice carving contest in the park and sledding races on the hill by the high school. She secretly thought that some of the tourists in her deli hadn't come for the festival at all; they just wanted to stop by and speculate about the murder.

"Hey, you," a male voice said, distracting her from the mental math she was doing as she counted the customers and estimated how much soup they had left. They were running low on cheese, too; she would have to order another delivery soon.

"Oh, hi," she said when she looked up and recognized Marcus. "How are you doing?"

"I am doing well," he said. "And you?"

"Busy," she told him with a tired smile. "But that's a good thing."

"I can see that. I won't hold you up for long; I was just in town and figured I would stop by." He grinned at her. "Plus, I wanted to make sure you hadn't changed your mind about going to the dance with me."

"Of course not." She smiled at him. "I'm looking forward to it."

"In that case," he said, returning her smile. "I would like a bowl of your soup, and then I will be on my way."

"Which one?" she asked. "We have Tuscan bean chili, and creamy lemon chicken soup."

"Surprise me," he told her. She was just turning away to go get the soup for him when she saw someone shove his way angrily out of line and stalk out of the restaurant, slamming the door behind him. It was Steven, the man who had asked her to the dance first, and who she had turned down. She felt bad that he had overheard her and Marcus's conversation; even though she didn't particularly like him, she didn't want him to be hurt. *Oh, well,* she thought. *There's nothing I can do now.*

She returned a few moments later with a bowl of the chili for Marcus—it was her favorite of the two—and bade him a warm goodbye before turning to the next customer.

Luckily, they had enough soup to last through the rest of the evening, though they ran out of cookies part way through the day. She entertained the idea of adding cookies to the list of things that she offered daily; they seemed to be popular. However, she decided that she just didn't like baking enough to make a fresh batch every morning. Perhaps she could offer muffins on Sundays, or begin offering a wider assortment of freshly baked bread. She made a mental note to see if any of her employees other than Candice were handy with baking, and if they would be willing to put in a few extra hours a week to help with it.

"Ms. Darling, someone left these for you," Dante told her when she came out of the kitchen for the last time. He was holding a bouquet of red roses. Her heart skipped a beat when she saw them as she recalled the rose that had been on the food critic's body and the one that David said had been dropped next to him when he was attacked.

"Do you know who they're from?" she asked warily.

"No, sorry, neither of us saw who dropped them off —it must have been during the busiest part of the day, right before close. Darrin found them on one of the tables over there." He inclined his head towards the front of the room where there were a few small bistro tables.

"Are you sure they're for me?" She took the flowers cautiously, half expecting something bad to happen. Nothing did.

"Yeah, there's a note with your name on it." She looked and saw that there indeed was. It read *For Moira* in slanted handwriting. "Who do you think left them?" he asked.

"I don't know," she said. "It could be Marcus. It's probably Marcus. He must have gone to get flowers, and when he came back and saw how busy we were, he didn't want to interrupt."

She was trying to convince herself as she said it, but the words didn't ring quite true. Marcus could easily have walked up and handed the flowers to whoever was at the register, or at least put them on the counter. He didn't seem like a shy man, and she thought he would probably have signed the note with his name. Besides, she hardly knew him; they were going to the dance together because they were both single and they had a friend in common. They seemed to get along well enough, but there wasn't really any romance between them—not yet, anyway. They didn't know each other well enough for that. She just hoped that they weren't from Johan, in some misguided attempt to either apologize to her for his behavior the other night, or to try to woo her further.

"That's nice of him," her employee said, obviously not as curious about them as she was, now that she had given him a reasonable solution to who they were from. "Do you need any more help here tonight?"

"Nope, I'm just going to mop the floors, and then I'll call it a night," she told him, putting the mystery of the flowers out of her mind temporarily. There was work to do, and the flowers would still be there in an hour when she was home and could call David. "You and Darrin can get going. Oh, and you can leave right after lunch tomorrow if you want, since it's Valentine's Day." She didn't know if he had a girl-friend, but she thought she would offer anyway. She was closing early on the night of the dance, so she wouldn't be there alone for more than a couple of hours.

"Thanks, Ms. Darling. I'll take you up on that." He shot her a grin, and then ducked into the kitchen to grab his coat and tell Darrin that they were free to go.

At home, later that night, Moira called David. She was relieved to hear that he sounded much better, if a bit spacey. He had taken the day off, and spent most of it taking things easy and recovering. He still didn't have any leads about the identity of the attacker, but he told her that both the Lake Marion and Maple Creek police were working on the case. He had informed them about the single red rose found at the scenes of both crimes, and they said that they would look into it. That brought Moira to her main reason for calling him so late, the thing that had been on her mind the entire evening; the bouquet of roses that had mysteriously appeared at the deli.

"They could be from Marcus," she said. "But it just seems like too big of a coincidence."

"Marcus?" David asked. Moira realized that she hadn't told him about her date yet.

"Oh, he's a friend of Martha's. He asked me to the Valentine's dance at City Hall," she said.

"You're going with him?" he asked. She thought for a moment that she heard a note of disappointment in his voice, but dismissed it. He was still out of it from his injuries and the pain meds.

"Yeah, I agreed to it even though I don't know him that well. I don't go out that often. It should be nice," she paused. "So, do you think I'm overreacting and the roses *are* from him?"

"I don't know. It's possible, but like you said, that would be quite the coincidence. Couldn't you just ask him?"

"I will tomorrow," she told him. "It's late, and I don't know much about his schedule."

"Well, keep me updated. And be careful, Moira. I have the feeling that whatever is going on, you're at the center of it."

THIRTEEN

She was woken from her dreams by an insistent ringing. At first she thought it was her alarm, and that she had somehow slept in late, but it was still dark outside. She realized that the sound was her cell phone ringing, which never meant anything good in the middle of the night. Sitting bolt upright so suddenly that the blanket fell off her, she grabbed her phone to see Martha's name on the screen. She answered it cautiously, not sure what to expect.

"Moira, thank goodness you answered." Her friend's voice was panicked, and Moira's heart lurched. Something bad must have happened.

"What's wrong?" she asked in concern.

"It's Marcus. He's in the hospital."

"Oh, my goodness, what happened?" Her first thought was that he must have been in some sort of car accident. It seemed to be a bad week for the men that she knew.

"He was attacked. Someone stabbed him when he was getting out of his car this evening," Martha said, her voice shaky.

"How bad is it?" Moira asked, feeling faint.

"Pretty bad," the other woman said honestly. "He's in surgery now. The doctor said he didn't think the knife hit any major organs, so that's good, I guess. Luckily someone saw it happen and called an ambulance. They guy who attacked him ran away when they shouted."

"Does anyone know who stabbed him or why?" she asked, her mind racing.

"No. The person was wearing a ski mask, and Marcus was too out of it to say anything."

"Was there a red rose at the scene of the crime?"

"Well... yes," Martha said after a pause. "The guy dropped one when he ran away. How did you know that?"

"Because David got attacked by a man in a ski mask the other day, and the guy left a rose there as well," she said grimly. "Which means that the attacker must be the same person."

"Is he okay? What happened?"

Moira told her the story, and then asked her friend to give her best wishes to Marcus, and to let her know when he was out of surgery. She was still in shock when she got off the phone, and lay in bed for a long time without closing her eyes. Someone had attacked David and Marcus and had killed Jason Platte. All three were men that she knew to varying degrees, but in such a small town, it could be coincidence. Especially since as she owned the only deli in town, she'd seen most people at least once.

Unable to sleep, she got up and wandered down to the kitchen for a midnight snack. She worried about David and Marcus, and couldn't help feeling that she was somehow responsible for the fact that they had both been attacked. As she raised a glass of water to her lips, she glanced out the kitchen window and froze. Under the streetlight in front of her house a car was idling. She could see its exhaust rising in steamy plumes.

She didn't recognize the car and it was impossible to see who was in it from this angle, but something about it made the hair on the back of her neck stand up. Even though there were plenty of other houses on the street, she couldn't shake the feeling that whoever was in the car was watching hers.

Moira shut off the kitchen light and pulled a chair up to the window, confident that no one would be able to see inside her dark house from that far away. Water and cookie forgotten, she watched the car, her discomfort rising with each minute that passed. No one would just sit there and waste fuel for that long without a good reason, would they? Even if someone was watching her house, it couldn't be so terribly interesting as to justify them sitting there for so long in the middle of the night.

Should I call the police? she wondered. As far as she knew, it wasn't illegal for whoever was in the car to just sit there. For all she knew, it was someone on a road trip who had simply pulled onto a quiet street to take a nap before continuing on in a few hours.

The police wouldn't appreciate the waste of their time, and the car wasn't really hurting anyone, so once her eyes began to droop she left her vigil at the window and trudged upstairs to bed.

In the morning she had a couple of texts from Martha telling her that Marcus was out of surgery and was recovering well. Glad that he was going to be okay, she sent a text back asking if it would be all right to call him at the hospital later. Then she phoned David, who sounded much better this morning than he had the day before, though his cheery mood didn't last long when she told him what had happened the night before.

"I'll call the detective that's working my case and let him know as soon as we get off the phone," he told her. "Though I'm sure he's aware of it, it won't hurt to cross-check the facts that we have. Whoever is doing this has proved their willingness to kill, and I don't want to have to find out the hard way who they have their sights on next."

This reminded Moira of the car that had been watching her house the night before. It seemed like a foggy dream now that it was morning with sunlight streaming in the window, and she thought that she had probably been overreacting last night. She hadn't exactly been in her right mind, after all. She didn't tell David about it, but she did go check to see if the car was still there once she got off the phone with him. It was gone, and she breathed a sigh of relief until she saw something lying in the snow near where the car had been parked. Unable to see clearly what it was from her window, she pulled her boots on and went outside in her bathrobe, her heart pounding faster and faster as she neared the object. It was a single rose, blood red against the white snow.

FOURTEEN

Moira was glad that it was another busy day at the deli. She didn't even mind all of the questions from people who seemed fascinated by the fact that there had been a dead guy, and a fairly well known dead guy at that, in the store just a week ago. The conversations helped to distract her from thinking of the person who had attacked David and Marcus and killed Jason Platte sitting outside her window all night. She had hardly been able to convince herself to go into work alone that morning, but after checking the recording from the security camera the night before and double-checking that nothing had triggered the motion detector, she thought that the deli was probably safe.

Since Marcus was in the hospital, she was no longer planning on going to the dance. She hadn't particularly wanted to go in the first place, and with her date injured, though recovering, it wouldn't feel right. Instead, she would spend the evening with David, trying to figure out who was behind the attacks. Though she had entertained the idea that Denise Donovan was behind it, she just couldn't make all of the connections. Yes, the woman might have had motive to kill the food critic if she had somehow known that he was giving her a bad review, but Denise was new to the area and as far as Moira knew, she didn't know either Marcus or David. With nothing to connect them and no motive, she thought that she could safely cross Denise off her list of possible suspects. The problem was, the list was very small. In fact, Denise had been the only person on it. There just wasn't enough evidence for Moira to suspect anyone else, and with so many tourists in town, it could be nearly anyone.

She said goodbye to Dante shortly after three so that he could get ready for whatever he was doing for Valentine's Day. She knew that Candice would be busy preparing for the dance, and Darrin was likely going to be attending as well, though he hadn't mentioned whether he had a date. She was closing the deli in another two hours; once the light parade and the dance started, there was no point in being open. Time passed slowly, with small rushes of customers and long lulls in between. Everyone was excited, and most people who stopped in were only there to buy last minute groceries that they might need over the weekend. No one was buying any of the fresh food, since the dance would have free snacks and drinks.

As evening began to fall, fewer and fewer people came in. The floors had long since been swept and mopped, and all of the goods were straightened on the shelves. The dishes were done, other than the still-simmering pots of soup, and the windows were sparkling. With nothing left to do, Moira took a seat behind the counter and began playing with the security camera app on her phone. It was neat to be able to watch herself sitting there and even more interesting to access the storage files and watch what had gone on earlier in the day. She couldn't believe that she hadn't installed anything like this before; with this technology, she would be able to keep an eye on the deli no matter where she was, as long as she had her phone. She could even go back and access old files from up to a week before.

An idea occurred to her so suddenly that she nearly dropped her phone. The security camera recorded everything, all the time, unlike the motion detector, which was only active during the hours the store was closed. That meant that the camera would have recorded whoever had dropped off the flowers. She had never gotten a chance to ask Marcus about them, so there was still a chance that he had done it, in which case she wouldn't be any closer to finding out who the killer was. Unless he was the killer and had knifed himself to keep the eyes of the police off of him... but no, that didn't make sense. For one, he would have had no reason to attack David or to kill Jason. Plus, while Marcus was unconscious in the hospital, someone *had* been watching her from a car last night; that person *had* left a red rose which linked him—or her—to the other crimes.

Her heart pounding with excitement, and trying not to be angry at herself for taking so long to come up with the idea, she found the correct date in the app's storage and began playing the video. Since she had no idea what time the flowers had been dropped off, it took her a while to find the right moment. She had been looking for Johan, but when she finally saw a man walk through the front door with a bouquet of roses in his hands, she paused the video and stared at his face. The image was grainy, but she thought she recognized his sandy blonde hair and glasses. It was Steven, the man that had asked her to the dance last Sunday.

She played the video long enough to watch him place the roses on a table and walk away before she set down her phone and stared numbly at the image of him on his way out the door. *This isn't necessarily solid evidence that he's the killer*, she thought, trying to convince herself that there could be another explanation. Then she stopped trying to give Steven the benefit of the doubt; there could only be so many coincidences. Steven had been there when she and Marcus were discussing their date for the dance, and he had been visibly upset. A few hours later, Marcus had been stabbed. He had also been there on the day that David had stayed to help her at the deli for a few hours, and the private detective had been attacked a day later.

But what about the food critic? Why would Steven kill him? He seemed to have been targeting men that were close to her, and she had been anything but close to Jason. She frowned, trying to remember each time she had seen the suspected killer. Had he been there when she and Martha were talking about the bad review that Jason Platte had given her last year? She thought so, though she hadn't known Steven's name at the time. He might have heard Martha's concerns about the deli losing business.

The one thing that she couldn't understand was why Steven would try to hurt people that she was close to. She barely knew him, and had only spoken to him a handful of times. If she was right and he *was* the killer, then she supposed that the why didn't matter that much right now. What mattered was turning him in before he could hurt anyone else.

She had just made the decision to call the police when the deli's front door swung open, letting in a cold gust of wind. She looked up, hurriedly arranging her face into what she hoped was a normal expression so as not to frighten the customer, but froze halfway through the motion. Steven was standing in the doorway, a single red rose clutched in his hand.

Quickly forcing herself to smile, she offered what she hoped was a cheery greeting. She didn't know what Steven was there for, but she knew that if he knew that she had found out the truth, then she was in more danger than she had ever been in before. Her only hope was to act like she had no idea that he had attacked two of her friends and killed someone else, and she didn't know if she was a good enough actor to achieve that. She was certain that he would be able to read the truth in her eyes.

"How can I help you?" she asked, relieved that her voice didn't shake.

"I saw your car in the lot, and thought I'd stop in," he replied. "You shouldn't be alone on Valentine's Day."

"I'm not here for much longer; we close in just a few minutes. Thanks for the concern, though." Her voice sounded hollow even to herself. "What can I get you?"

"Let me see…" His eyes drifted towards the menu for a moment, and then down to the plate of cookies, half of which still remained. She saw her phone lying next to the plate too late. The screen was still on, and the image of Steven leaving the deli was as clear as day. Her blood turning to ice, she risked a glance back up at him and knew that he had seen it, too.

The second his eyes met hers and she saw the cold rage in them, she ran. He was between her and the front door, so she went the only direction she could— into the kitchen. The door between the kitchen and the front room didn't have a lock on it, so she only got a few steps into the room before Steven burst through after her. His eyes were wild. Frozen in terror, she watched as he slipped a knife from his pocket. The rose dropped from his hand to the floor, and one of the petals came off and slowly followed the flower down, floating the rest of the way until it came to rest on top of his boot. She saw all of this with strange clarity, as if it were happening in slow motion. She kept telling herself to run, to try to make it to the side door, but his gaze had her pinned in place. If she moved, time might start again, and then he would kill her.

She slid her eyes over to the counter where her purse was, and despaired that the pepper spray was so far away. It was halfway between them, what seemed like a hopeless distance away, but it was open and she knew exactly which pocket the pepper spray was in.

Trying not to think about it too much, she made a sudden lunge towards the purse. Steven was faster, and caught her roughly by the upper arm. His fingers dug into her skin, sure to leave bruises if she survived this.

"Let me go," she gasped, recoiling automatically, which just made him dig his fingers in even more tightly.

"You should have just said yes," he hissed at her, ignoring her demand. "All I wanted to do was take you to the dance."

"I don't understand why you're doing this." She couldn't take her eyes off the knife in his hand.

"I love you," he said. "I did everything I could for you. I killed for you. But still you just couldn't do something as simple as go on one date with me." He jerked her closer. "It's always the same with you women. No matter how much I do, it's never enough."

"What do you mean, you killed for me?" she managed to say, frantically looking around for anything that she could use to save herself.

"The man who unfairly judged the deli, I killed him. I heard you and your friend talk about the review maybe putting you out of business." His grip tightened. "I was protecting you."

"What about David, and Marcus?" she asked, doing her best to stall.

"They shouldn't have gotten involved with you," he said with a snort of disgust. "Enough talking. You've had your chances. You're just like all the others. I shouldn't have wasted my time on you."

Moira saw his grip tighten on the knife, and knew that the end was near. He was too strong, there was no way she could break free from his grip. Her pepper spray was out of reach in her purse, and her cell phone was in the front room. There was nothing within reach that could save her. Nothing except... her eyes landed on the still-simmering pots of soup on the stove.

She made her move just as Steven was bringing the knife up. Her hand closed firmly around the nearest pot's handle. As quickly as she could, she jerked it off the stove and flung the contents at him, the pot, too, for good measure. With a strangled cry of agony as scalding-hot soup splashed across his face, he let her go. Before he had a chance to recover, she leapt past him and dashed through the swinging door to the front room, where her phone was still sitting next to the plate of cookies. She grabbed it and dialed the police as she ran out of the building, not caring that it was freezing outside. She didn't stop until she heard the howling of the sirens and a saw a patrol unit pull up next to her.

FIFTEEN

"Are you sure you don't want me to take you home?" David asked, his eyes soft as he watched her.

"No. I need to clean up," she told him. Realizing that her hands were still shaking, she sat down in a chair. "Though I might sit here for a little bit first."

"You're sure he didn't hurt you?"

"Just a few bruises. I'm fine." She managed a shaky laugh. "I'm exhausted and shaken up, but fine."

Thanks to the quick response of the police, Steven, still covered in soup, had been caught red-handed only a block away from the deli. The security camera had caught enough of the incident that there were no doubts about whether Moira's story was true. The police had questioned her and, after making sure she was okay, had left her in peace. Tomorrow she would have to go down to the station to make a formal statement, but for the moment, she and David were alone.

David had come quickly when she had called him even though she hadn't managed to tell the full story over the phone. She had been shocked to see the bruises on his face from when Steven had attacked him, and felt immense guilt that he had gotten hurt because of her.

"Some Valentine's Day, huh?" she joked weakly.

"At least it's over," he told her, glancing at his watch. "It's officially the fifteenth."

"Thank goodness." She buried her head in her hands. "I'm not looking forward to telling Candice what happened. Or Darrin and Dante, for that matter. They'll be so concerned."

"You don't have to do any of that until you get some rest." He stood up. "I'll go put some coffee on, and then I'll help you clean up the spilled soup. After that, I'll drive you home. Candice can help you get your car tomorrow."

"Thank you so much," she said sincerely. "You don't have to do any of this, you know. I'd be able to manage on my own—don't feel like you have to stay and help."

"Nonsense," he said, giving her a small smile. "There isn't anywhere I would rather be." She could tell by the look in his eyes that he meant it. She smiled at him. He was a good friend, but something about his words made her think that he might want to be more.

"Let's get started," she said, standing up. She was too tired to think about David and their feelings towards each other at the moment. She had so much left to do, and knew that she would be busier than ever for the next few weeks. Besides repairing the damage from tonight, she would have to make amends with Denise at some point. Her husband may not have been the murderer, but he still acted like a slimebag. Women had to stick together, and the two of them had enough in common that they might even become good friends. "The sooner we get done, the sooner I can go to bed and wake up to a new, and hopefully better, day."

***

If you enjoyed Cold Cut Murder, check out the next book in the series, Grilled Cheese Murder, today!

Made in the USA
Las Vegas, NV
21 June 2024

91327948R00066